Curious George

and Friends

Favorite Stories
by Margret & H. A. Rey

 Houghton Mifflin Company Boston 2003

With appreciation to Lay Lee Ong,
Emily West, and Norman West

www.houghtonmifflinbooks.com

Contents

Memories of the Reys

By lucky chance Hans Rey's niece was in New York City when I first arrived in May 1943. A mutual friend had asked her to look me up. I had just graduated from the University of Toronto in art history and had a student visa to attend summer classes at the Art Students League. I hoped to stay on in New York and illustrate children's books. So when Lottie said she would introduce me to her aunt and uncle, Margret and Hans Rey, who were in that field, I was delighted.

Although I had never heard of the Reys, I soon discovered that they were well known. They had come from Germany via France and Brazil in 1940 and already had had several books published in the United States, as well as in France and England.

The Reys lived in Greenwich Village, as I did, and life there was casual and fun. Washington Square, where they lived, was a great meeting place, and the Reys knew lots of people—friends and authors and artists from all over. Margret was the more gregarious; Hans was quieter, with a smile for everyone. Most of the people they knew had dogs and walked them every evening in the square. Margret and Hans had a black cocker spaniel, Charkie, the first of a succession of spaniels. When Charkie got old and his whiskers turned white, people would say, "Poor old dog." Margret soon stopped such remarks by dyeing his whiskers black. The Reys' dogs were an important part of their life, and Hans sometimes put Margret and Charkie in his illustrations, as in *The Park Book* and *Curious George Rides a Bike*.

I had no experience in book illustration, and no samples or portfolio. When I asked the Reys for advice, Hans, who was always kind and helpful, encouraged me to make some samples. This was fortunate, because one day in 1948 Margret called and said that Ursula Nordstrom at Harper, one of the best children's book editors in the business, had asked if she knew any new artists for a new book, and Margret recommended me. So I began my career with Harper.

The Reys had a charming, light, and airy third-floor studio apartment overlooking the trees in Washington Square. Whenever I visited them

I would see books being created: sketches, pieces of type, and dummies spread all over. Generally the books began with one of Hans's great pictorial ideas, such as the soap powder episode in *Curious George Gets a Medal.*

Hans's drawings have a wonderful vitality, a feeling of life and motion and fun. When the Boston Public Library had a big exhibit of the Reys' work in 2000, I was thrilled to see a very early drawing, done when Hans was eight, of people riding in a park in Hamburg. The horses move and prance, and one realizes how obvious his talent was from the beginning.

Margret was a gifted idea person, writer, and editor; she was very like Curious George, mischievous and inquisitive. Hans and Margret were a perfect picture-book team. Together they constructed the story amid lots of arguments and changes. Sometimes Margret would quickly take a sketch from Hans, cut it up, and put it together in a more dramatic way. Margret could be very critical, as all who met her soon found out. Both Reys were meticulous craftsmen: each page was carefully designed and every detail thoroughly worked out. Hans did four-color separations of the artwork: each color had to be interpreted in black and gray on a separate sheet of paper, a difficult and demanding task.

In 1963 Margret and Hans moved to Cambridge, Massachusetts, and spent summers in Waterville Valley, New Hampshire. Living close to Harvard Square, the Reys lived very much as they had in New York. Cambridge in the 1960s was similar to the Village in the 1940s and '50s. There were get-togethers with friends and relatives, dog walking, socializing in the street, visits to bookshops and art galleries, concerts and parties. The Reys always gave a New Year's Eve party with champagne and beautiful hors d'oeuvres lovingly made by Hans. In Cambridge they had a large house and a small garden; in Waterville Valley, a small house and a large garden. Margret was an avid and enthusiastic gardener; she was always busy and cheerful, singing as she dug and planted. She was also an enthusiastic potter, taking lessons at the Cambridge Center for Adult Education and the Haystack Mountain School of Crafts in Maine.

Hans's passion was astronomy; he wrote two very successful books: *The Stars: A New Way to See Them* and *Find the Constellations*, a star book for children. He had clever new ideas and made excellent, easy-to-read star charts. He always had a telescope at hand and loved showing people the stars. In Cambridge he would set up his telescope in front of the house and invite the neighbors to take a look. He always had a cluster of fascinated people around him. It was the same in Waterville Valley, where the clear night skies delighted him.

When I moved to Cambridge in the summer of 1965, I was working on the first book that I both wrote and illustrated, *Be Nice to Spiders*, about a spider named Helen. Before the Reys went to Waterville for the summer, I showed the dummy to Margret and asked for her advice. She sent me the following:

> Re: Helen: I think you are doing alright. You just have to learn how to put a story together. A story should always have a hero (Helen) whom you can identify with, or let's say, feel with. And it should come to a climax, the climax in your case being that Helen nearly gets killed when they clean up. Maybe it needs a scene, picture, when they clean up and nearly get her with the broom. And then an ending, in this case the discovery that Helen is doing good, plus an end picture which should come quickly, not an ending that is drawn out too long. Well— that's the way I see it, but I guess I said that all before.

I came to know the Reys much better after I moved to Cambridge. They were a great and lasting influence on my life, and I am eternally grateful to them both.

—MARGARET BLOY GRAHAM
  Cambridge, Massachusetts
  July 2002

Curious George

by

H. A. Rey

This is George.
He lived in Africa.
He was a good little monkey
and always very curious.

One day George saw a man.
He had on a large yellow straw hat.
The man saw George too.
"What a nice little monkey," he thought.
"I would like to take him home with me."
He put his hat on the ground
and, of course, George was curious.
He came down from the tree
to look at the large yellow hat.

The hat had been on the man's head.
George thought it would be nice
to have it on his own head.
He picked it up and put it on.

The hat covered George's head.
He couldn't see.
The man picked him up quickly
and popped him into a bag.
George was caught.

The man with the big yellow hat
put George into a little boat,
and a sailor rowed them both
across the water to a big ship.
George was sad, but he was still
a little curious.

On the big ship, things began to happen.
The man took off the bag.
George sat on a little stool and the man said,
"George, I am going to take you to a big Zoo
in a big city. You will like it there.
Now run along and play,
but don't get into trouble."
George promised to be good.
But it is easy for little monkeys to forget.

On the deck he found some sea gulls.
He wondered how they could fly.
He was very curious.
Finally he HAD to try.
It looked easy. But—

oh, what happened!
First this—

and then this!

"WHERE IS GEORGE?"
The sailors looked and looked.
At last they saw him
struggling in the water,
and almost all tired out.

"Man overboard!" the sailors cried
as they threw him a lifebelt.
George caught it and held on.
At last he was safe on board.

After that George was more careful
to be a good monkey, until, at last,
the long trip was over.
George said good-bye to the kind sailors,
and he and the man with the yellow hat
walked off the ship on to the shore
and on into the city to the man's house.

After a good meal
and a good pipe
George felt very tired.

He crawled into bed
and fell asleep at once.

The next morning
the man telephoned the Zoo.
George watched him.
He was fascinated.
Then the man went away.

George was curious.
He wanted to telephone, too.
One, two, three, four, five, six, seven.
What fun!

DING-A-LING-A-LING!
GEORGE HAD TELEPHONED
THE FIRE STATION!
The firemen rushed to the telephone.
"Hello! Hello!" they said.
But there was no answer.
Then they looked for the signal
on the big map that showed
where the telephone call had come from.
They didn't know it was GEORGE.
They thought it was a real fire.

HURRY! HURRY! HURRY!
The firemen jumped on to the fire engines
and on to the hook-and-ladders.
Ding-dong-ding-dong.
Everyone out of the way!
Hurry! Hurry! Hurry!

The firemen rushed into the house.
They opened the door.
NO FIRE!
ONLY a naughty little monkey.
"Oh, catch him, catch him," they cried.
George tried to run away.
He almost did, but he got caught
in the telephone wire, and —

a thin fireman caught one arm
and a fat fireman caught the other.
"You fooled the fire department,"
they said. "We will have to shut you up
where you can't do any more harm."
They took him away
and shut him in a prison.

George wanted to get out.
He climbed up to the window
to try the bars.
Just then the watchman came in.
He got on the wooden bed to catch George.
But he was too big and heavy.
The bed tipped up,
the watchman fell over,
and, quick as lightning,
George ran out through the open door.

He hurried through the building
and out on to the roof. And then
he was lucky to be a monkey:
out he walked on to the telephone wires.
Quickly and quietly over the guard's head,
George walked away.
He was free!

Down in the street
outside the prison wall,
stood a balloon man.
A little girl bought a balloon
for her brother.
George watched.
He was curious again.
He felt he MUST have
a bright red balloon.
He reached over and
tried to help himself, but—

instead of one balloon,
the whole bunch broke loose.
In an instant
the wind whisked them all away
and, with them, went George,
holding tight with both hands.

Up, up he sailed, higher and higher.
The houses looked like toy houses
and the people like dolls.
George was frightened.
He held on very tight.

At first the wind blew in great gusts.
Then it quieted.
Finally it stopped blowing altogether.
George was very tired.
Down, down he went—bump,
on to the top of a traffic light.
Everyone was surprised.
The traffic got all mixed up.
George didn't know what to do,
and then he heard someone call,
"GEORGE!"
He looked down and saw his friend,
the man with the big yellow hat!

George was very happy.
The man was happy too.
George slid down the post
and the man with the big yellow hat
put him under his arm.
Then he paid the balloon man
for all the balloons.
And then George and the man
climbed into the car
and at last, away they went

to the ZOO!

What a nice place
for George to live!

Cecily G.
and the 9 monkeys

By
H. A. REY

Here are the names of the nine monkeys in this book:

Mother Pamplemoose and Baby Jinny

Curious George who was clever, too

James who was good

Johnny who was brave

Arthur who was kind

David who was strong

and Punch and Judy, the twins

This is Cecily G. Her whole name is Cecily Giraffe, but she is called Cecily G. or just plain Cecily for short.

One day she was very sad because all her family and all her friends had been taken away to a zoo. Cecily G. was all alone. She began to cry because she wanted someone to play with.

Now, in another place,
lived a mother monkey called
Mother Pamplemoose and eight little monkeys. They
were sad, too, because some woodcutters had cut down
all the trees in their forest, and monkeys have to have
trees to live in. One of the little monkeys was called
Curious George. He was a clever monkey. He said,
"We must pack up at once and go on a journey to find
a new home."

So they did. They walked and they walked and they
walked until they came to the bank of a deep river. They
couldn't get across and there wasn't any way around.
They didn't know *what* to do.

Suddenly Jinny, the baby monkey, pointed across to the other bank.

There stood Cecily Giraffe! When she saw the monkeys, she stopped crying. "Do you want to get across?" she said.

"Yes, yes!" they cried.

"Step back then," called Cecily G.

Yoop! With one big jump Cecily's front feet landed on the monkeys' side of the bank. And then she stood still.

Curious George was the first to see that Cecily had made herself into a bridge. He ran across. Then came Johnny, who was a brave monkey. Then all the others, one by one.

"Thank you, dear Giraffe," shouted George, "and please put your head down a little so that we can talk to you without shouting. That's better! What is your name and why are you sad?"

"My name is Cecily Giraffe, and I am unhappy because I haven't anyone to play with. Why are *you* sad?"

"We are sad," said George, "because we haven't anywhere to live."

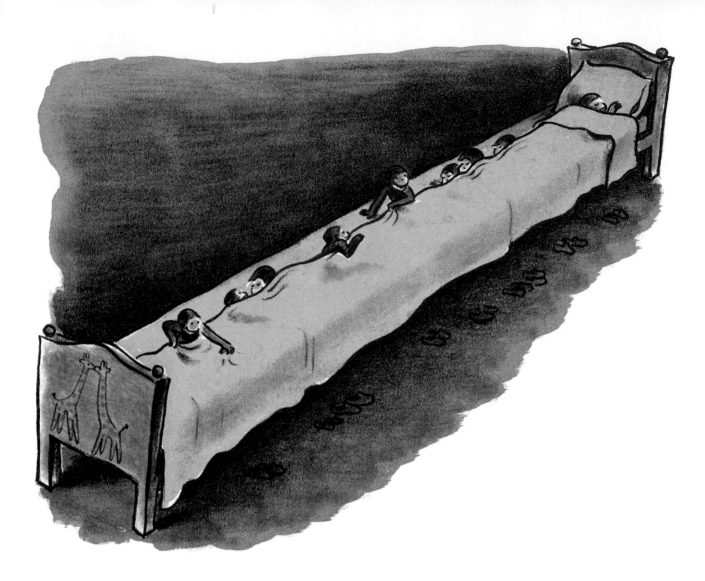

"Then why don't you stay with me for a while?" said
Cecily. "My house is empty now."

"We'd love to," cried all the monkeys at once.

"Good!" said Cecily, and she smiled for the first time
that day. "Now it is bedtime. I'll show you your room,
and tomorrow we'll have some lovely games." So she
tucked all the nine monkeys into one giraffe bed, and
in a few minutes they were fast asleep.

Next morning, after a good night's sleep and a big breakfast, Cecily G. said, "Now let's play see-saw! James, you sit on my back. (James was a very good monkey and usually had first turn.) George, you climb on my head, and you, Johnny, sit on my hind feet. That's the way!"

"Now," they cried, "off we go!" Cecily stood up on her front legs. Up-down, up-down, up-down, went the see-saw.

After a while Cecily stopped and took on another load. Everyone had a turn; but baby Jinny got so excited that Mother Pamplemoose was afraid she would fall off. She had to climb down and give her place to James, who got an extra ride. Jinny cried a little, but Arthur, who was very kind, dried her tears and told her that he had an idea for another game that she could play better.

So Arthur whispered something to all the other monkeys. They rushed into the house where they had left their belongings and in a minute they were back with their skis.

"But there isn't any snow for skis," said Cecily G.

"Please," said George, "be so kind as to stretch your neck so I can tie your head to the top of that palm tree over there."

"I'll be glad to," said Cecily, and she did.

Then all the monkeys put on their skis, climbed the tree, and slid down Cecily's back, over and over again. Brave Johnny even did stunts. When he jumped he seemed to be flying.

After a while Cecily's neck got tired, but she was having such a good time that she hardly noticed. "You are a wonderful skier, Johnny," she said.

Johnny was so pleased he tried a specially high jump and — bump — down he fell, flat on his nose.

Mother Pamplemoose ran to pick him up. "I think it is time to play something else," she said. "Let's find a game that Cecily can play too."

"Yes, yes," cried all the monkeys.

Johnny thought very hard because he was such a good monkey that he wanted Cecily to be sure and have fun, too. All at once he had a wonderful idea. "We'll make some *stilts* for Cecily G.," he cried.

Johnny and David, who was a very strong monkey, cut down two palm trees. The twins, Punch and Judy, did the sawing.

James hammered the nails.

George watched and gave advice. When the stilts were done, he proudly carried them to Cecily G. and showed her how to use them.

Cecily Giraffe was terribly excited.

All the monkeys helped and — up — UP — UP — she went — right into the sky —

so high the page isn't big enough to show all of her.

It was very hot the next day and they all thought it
would be just the thing to go to the seashore.

After a short walk, they came to the beach and Mother
Pamplemoose thought it would be nice to have a swim
before lunch. But Johnny had been thinking. He asked
Cecily to put down her head so that he could whisper
in her ear.

Can you guess what he said? He wanted Cecily to
be a—

SAILBOAT! And so Cecily made herself into a sailboat. Johnny was Captain. He shouted orders and

80

pulled the ropes. "Not so hard, not so hard!" cried
Cecily. But she was too late —

over they went, into the water.

"Quick, quick, climb on my back," called Cecily Giraffe, when Johnny cried for help.

In a minute they were safe on the beach, but Cecily was so wet and cold, they decided to take off her skin and hang it in the sun to dry.

"It is quite complicated to be a giraffe," said Punch to Judy as they brought Cecily the clothespins.

Cecily Giraffe had hardly gotten her skin back on again when a big black cloud came up and hid the sun.

"Oh — oh — it's going to rain —" cried the monkeys.

Off they rushed, and back they came, one-two, one-two, carrying their umbrellas on their shoulders.

But the rain didn't start at once and James thought it would be fun to use the umbrellas for a new game. He called it "Parachute-jumping."

Each monkey, one at a time, climbed up on Cecily's head, opened his umbrella and jumped off.

Down they floated. It was such fun they did it hundreds of times.

All went well until, all of a sudden,
Curious George tipped his umbrella
sideways to see something and —
thump — down he fell. When
he looked at his broken
umbrella, he sat down on
the ground to cry. And,
just at that moment, the
rain started. Poor George!
Great splashing drops began
to fall all around him.

"Quick, quick, climb
up my neck, George,"
said Cecily.

George climbed up and up until he was in the sun-
shine again, high above the rain cloud.

All week long Cecily and her new friends had great fun. When Sunday came, Cecily was so happy she decided to give a concert to celebrate. The monkeys thought it a splendid idea. Arthur made up a nice song for them all to sing together and George promised to play on the harp.

At last they were ready and George was just starting
them off when someone cried —

"Fire! Fire! Cecily's house is burning!"

The concert stopped almost before it started, but no one knew what to do to put out the fire.

"If only we had a ladder, we could throw water on the flames," cried Mother Pamplemoose.

"I know what to do," said James. "There's a pump near the house, and a hose, and Cecily can be the ladder."

Punch and Judy worked the pump and ——

George climbed up to turn the hose on the fire. James
stood on Cecily's back to guide the hose up to George.

In a minute the fire was out and Cecily's house was saved.

Cecily looked at the wet little monkeys and said, "Dear new friends, I don't know how to thank you. . . . Would you like to stay with me always? It would make me very happy."

"Oh, Cecily G.," cried Mother Pamplemoose, baby Jinny, curious George, brave Johnny, good little James, kind Arthur, strong David, and the twins, Punch and Judy, all together, "We'll stay with you for ever and ever. . . . And now let's finish our concert."

So they took hold of hands, danced round in a ring

and sang Arthur's song as loud as they could sing.

Nine lit-tle monks were we home-less and

in di-is - may till Ce-ci - ly Gi-

raff' had us a - long t-o stay

so here in a ri-ing we'll all dance and si-ing

Cec'-ly Cec'-ly we will ne-ver go a-way.

ELIZABITE

ADVENTURES OF
A CARNIVOROUS PLANT

by

H. A. REY

YOU would not think that plants like meat.
Well, some plants do. They catch and eat
Small insects, such as flies and ants,
And they are called

CARNIVOROUS PLANTS.

One of them came to world-wide fame;
ELIZABITE, that was her name.

Elizabite smiles at the sky
While a mosquito passes by.

Right in the middle of its flight
She captures it with great delight.

Elizabite smiles at the sky . . .
There comes another passer-by.

It's Doctor White, a scientist,
And well-known as a botanist.

"This plant is very rare indeed!
I'll take her home and get the seed."

"She's caught me—Ouch!" cries Doctor White,
"I did not know this plant could bite."

He now tries out a safer way,
And he succeeds without delay.

Victorious he leaves the place,
A smile of triumph on his face.

Here in the doctor's laboratory
Continues the amazing story.

The plant, for once, behaves all right.
She gets a drink from Doctor White,

And even, as a special treat,
Frankfurters, for she's fond of meat.

But Scotty thinks with jealousy,
Frankfurters should belong to ME!

Alas, it never pays to steal!
Elizabite will spoil his meal.

A sudden snap—a cry—a wail—
And there goes Scotty minus tail!

Mary, the maid, comes with her broom
To tidy up the messy room

And, unsuspecting, turns her back:
A tempting aim for an attack!

Elizabite's bad deeds require
A solid fence of strong barbed wire.

And Doctor White reports the case
Now to Professor Appleface.

But Appleface declares, "I doubt it
Till I myself find out about it."

He soon obtains the evidence
Despite the new barbed wire fence.

"We have to keep Elizabite
Chained to the kennel now," says White.

This burglar does not realize
The danger of his enterprise . . .

Next morning White perceives with fright
Someone inside Elizabite!

"How brave of her to catch this man!
Let's put him in the prison van."

Of course, Elizabite can't stay
With White. She now is on her way

To a new home, the nearby Zoo.

Here she became——and this is true——

At once the most outstanding sight.
Surrounded by her children bright
She lived in happiness and glory
Up to this day...

Here ends the story.

Margret Rey

Pretzel

With Pictures by H. A. Rey

One morning in May
five little dachshunds were born.

Pretzel

One of them was Pretzel.
They grew up the way puppies do, and they
all looked exactly alike the first few weeks.

Paul

Patricia

Priscilla

Percival

But after nine weeks Pretzel suddenly
started growing—
              and growing—
                         and growing.

He grew much longer than
any of his brothers and sisters.

And when he was fully grown
he had become the longest
dachshund in all the world.

Pretzel was very pleased with
himself because it is very distinguished
for a dachshund to be so long.

When he was one year old (a dachshund is grown up at that age) he won the Blue Ribbon at the Dog Show which means that everybody considered him the best looking dog of all.

All the dogs admired him.
And all the people admired him.

Only Greta didn't.

Greta was the little dachshund from
across the street. Pretzel was in love
with her and wanted to marry her.

But Greta just laughed at him.
　"I don't care for long dogs," she said.
　"But it is very distinguished
for a dachshund to be so long
and I won the Blue Ribbon at the
Dog Show," said Pretzel.
　"I still don't care," said Greta.
Pretzel was hurt but he did not show it.
　"Please marry me," he said,

"and I will do anything for you!"

"Prove it!" said Greta and went away.

So Pretzel set out to prove it. First
he brought Greta a nice big bone.

"Thanks for the bone," said Greta,
"but I won't marry you for that.
I don't care for long dogs." And
she ate the bone and forgot about
Pretzel.

Pretzel had to try something else. He gave her the lovely green rubber ball he had been given for his birthday.

"Thank you," said Greta, "but I still

won't marry you because I don't
care for long dogs. Besides, everybody
can give *presents!*" And she ran
away with the ball.

"Look what I can do! Nobody except me can do THAT!" said Pretzel when they met again.

And this is what he did:

"Not bad," said Greta. "Your name certainly fits you. But I like the pretzels at the baker's better, and I still don't care for long dogs." Pretzel was very unhappy.

Some weeks had passed and Greta hadn't even spoken to Pretzel. One day while she was playing with her green ball it bounced away. Greta tried to catch it and boomps! they both landed in a hole.

Greta tried to get out of the hole, but she couldn't. It was much too deep. She was terribly scared. If nobody came to save her she might never, never . . . Just then Pretzel's face appeared over the edge of the hole.

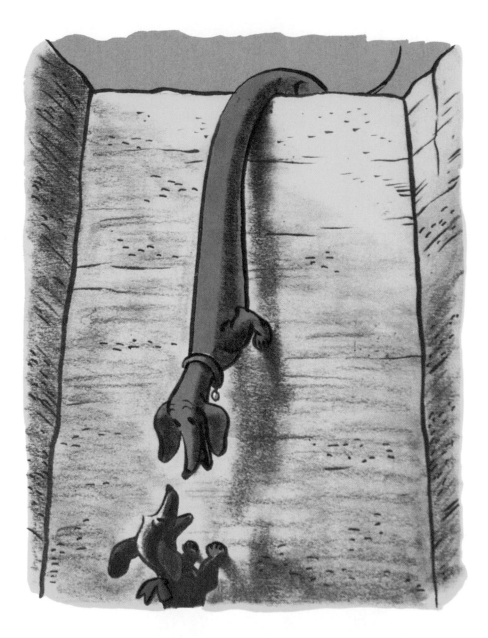

"I'll get you out of there!" he shouted.
(He had watched Greta all the time

and now had rushed to help her.)
How good that Pretzel was so long!

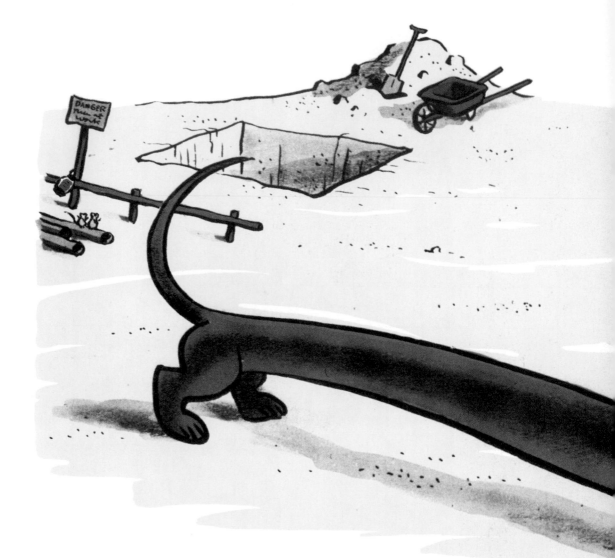

"I believe you saved my life. You are wonderful!" said Greta with a sigh.

"Will you marry me now?" asked Pretzel.
"I will," said Greta, "but not for your
length!" So they kissed each other,

and got married,

and one morning in May
five little dachshunds were born . . .

Emmy Payne

Katy
No-Pocket

Pictures by H. A. Rey

Big tears rolled down Katy Kangaroo's brown face. Poor Katy was crying because she didn't have a pocket like other mother kangaroos. Freddy was Katy Kangaroo's little boy and he needed a pocket to ride in. All grown-up kangaroos take awfully big hops and little kangaroos, like Freddy, get left far behind unless their mothers have nice pockets to carry them in.

And poor Katy didn't have any pocket at all.

Katy Kangaroo cried just thinking about it, and Freddy cried, too.

Then, all of a sudden, Katy had a wonderful idea! It was so wonderful she jumped six feet up in the air.

The idea was this. Other animal mothers had children and they didn't have any pockets. She'd go and ask one of them how they carried their babies!

Freddy looked all around to see whom to ask and Katy looked all around to see, too. And what they both saw were two bubbles rising up from the river right beside them.

"Mrs. Crocodile!" said Katy, feeling lots better already. "*She* hasn't any pocket. Let's ask her!"

A lot of big muddy bubbles came up through the water and

then Mrs. Crocodile stuck her head up and opened her *enormous* mouth and smiled.

"Why, Katy Kangaroo! What can I do for you today?"

"Please, Mrs. Crocodile, I am so sad," said Katy. "I have no pocket and Freddy has to walk wherever we go and he gets so tired. Oh dear, oh dear!"

And she started to cry again.

The crocodile began to cry, too, and then she said, "B-b–but — What — what can *I* do?"

"You can tell me how to carry Freddy," said Katy. "How do you carry little Catherine Crocodile? Oh, do *please* tell me."

"Why, I carry her on my back, of course!" said Mrs. Crocodile.

She was so surprised that anyone shouldn't know that she forgot to cry any more.

Katy was pleased. She said, "Thank you," and as soon as she got to a good squatting-down place, she squatted and said, "Now, Freddy, climb on my back. After this it will be so simple — no trouble at all."

But it wasn't simple. In the first place, Freddy could not crawl up onto her back because his knees stuck out. He couldn't hang on because his front legs were too short. And when he did manage to hang on for a few minutes and Katy gave a long hop, he fell off — bump, bang — with a terrific thump.

So Katy saw that she couldn't carry her baby on her back.

Katy and Freddy sat down again and thought and thought. "I know! I'll ask Mrs. Monkey. I'm sure she can help me."

So Katy and Freddy set off for the forest and very soon they found Mrs. Monkey. She had her young son, Jocko, with her and Katy Kangaroo hurried so to catch up with them that she was almost out of breath. But, finally, she managed to squeak, "Please, Mrs. Monkey, how do you carry Jocko?"

"Why, in my arms, of course," said Mrs. Monkey. "How else would any sensible animal carry anything?" And she whisked away through the trees.

"Oh dear," said Katy, and a great big tear ran across her long nose. "I can't carry anything in these short little arms, oh *dear!* She wasn't any help at all. What are we going to do?" And she just sat down and cried harder than ever.

Why in my arms, of course!

Poor Freddy! He hated to see his mother cry, so he put his paw to his head and he thought, and thought, and *thought*.

"What about the lion?" he asked when Katy stopped crying a little.

"They don't carry their children. The poor things walk just the way you do," said Katy.

the way the Lions do it

the way
the Birds do it

"There's — there's birds,"
said Freddy. "How do
they carry their babies?"

"Birds!" said Katy. "The mother birds push their children
out of the nest and they squawk and shriek and flap their
wings about it."

Then all at once Katy Kangaroo stopped crying and looked at Freddy. "They do say that the owl knows almost everything," she said slowly.

"Well, then, for goodness' sake, let's ask *him!*" said Freddy. They found the owl asleep in an old dead tree,

and he was cross because he didn't want to be waked up in the middle of the day. But when he saw that Katy was so sad he came out, blinking and ruffling his feathers and said in a scratchy voice, "Well! Well! what is it? Speak up! And speak loudly. I'm deaf as a post."

So Katy stood under the tree and screamed at him, "I'm a mother kangaroo and I haven't a pocket to carry my child in. How shall I carry him? What shall I do?"

"Get a pocket," said the owl and went to sleep again.

"Where?" cried Katy. "Oh, please, don't go to sleep before you tell me where!"

"How should I know?" said the owl. "They sell that sort of thing in the City, I believe. Now, kindly go away and let me sleep."

"The City!" said Katy, and looked at Freddy with big, round eyes. "Of course, we'll go to the City!"

Katy was so excited that
she almost left Freddy behind as she went leaping over
bushes and hopping along the path, singing in a sort of

hummy way a little song she had just made up:

"Hippity! Hoppity!
Flippity! Floppity!
Wasn't it a pity?
I didn't know
It was to the City
I should go!"

She hopped so fast that Freddy could hardly keep up, but at last they left the woods behind and came to the City

where there were stores and houses and automobiles.

The people all stared and stared at Katy, but she didn't notice it. She was looking for pockets and she saw that almost everybody had them.

And then, all at once, she saw — she could hardly believe it — a man who seemed to be ALL pockets! He was simply covered with pockets. Big pockets, little pockets, medium-sized pockets —

Katy went up to him and laid a paw on his arm. He was a little frightened, but Katy looked at him with her soft brown eyes and said, "Please, dear, kind man, where did you get all those pockets?"

"These pockets?" he said. "You want to know where I got all these pockets? Why, they just came with the apron, of course."

"You mean you can really get something to put on with ALL those pockets already in it?" asked Katy.

"Sure you can," said the man. "I keep my hammer and nails and tools in my pockets, but I can get another apron, so I'll give you mine."

He took off the apron

and dumped it UPSIDE DOWN. Out fell a saw, wrench, nails, a hammer, a drill, and lots of other tools. Then the man shook the apron hard and turned it right side up again and hung it around Katy's neck and tied it behind her back.

Katy was so pleased and excited and happy that she couldn't speak. She just stood still and looked down at the pockets and smiled and smiled and smiled.

By this time, a big crowd had gathered to see what Katy Kangaroo was doing. When they saw how pleased she was, they all smiled, too.

At last Katy was able to say "Thank you" to the nice, kind man, and then what do you think she did? She popped Freddy into a very comfortable pocket and she hippity-hopped home faster than ever before because, of course, she didn't have to wait for Freddy.

And when she got home, what do you think she did?

Well, she had so many pockets that she put Freddy into the biggest one of all. Then, into the next largest she put little Leonard Lion. Thomas Tortoise just fitted into another pocket.

Sometimes she had a baby bird if its mother was busy at a worm hunt. And there was still room for a monkey, a skunk, a rabbit, a raccoon, a lizard, a squirrel, a 'possum, a turtle, a frog, and a snail.

So now, all the animals
like Katy's pockets better than
any other pockets in the whole forest.

And Katy Kangaroo
is very happy because now
SHE HAS MORE POCKETS THAN
ANY MOTHER KANGAROO
IN THE WORLD!

The End

Margret Rey

Spotty

With Pictures by H. A. Rey

Mother Bunny and Aunt Eliza had a long talk. Mother Bunny was close to tears.

"How many did you say?" Aunt Eliza asked.

"Nine. Nine little bunnies, born last Friday. Eight of them look just the way all the others in the family look. Snow-white with pink eyes and pink ears. But the ninth . . ." Mother Bunny began to cry. "The ninth looks all different. He has brown spots all over and blue eyes. My poor little Spotty — I am so afraid that Grandpa may not like him. Grandpa has never known anything but white bunnies in the family. For him that's the way bunnies *should* be."

"I daresay this *is* a problem," Aunt Eliza said.

"Let's go and see them anyhow."

Nine little bunnies were happily munching leaves and chasing each other all over the woods.

"There is Spotty," Mother Bunny said.

"Why, of all things!" Aunt Eliza exclaimed, "brown spots all over! I have never seen such a thing!"

"Don't you like brown spots, Auntie?" Rosie asked. (She was playing nearby and had overheard the grownups talk.)

"I certainly don't," Aunt Eliza said. "Go and play now, Rosie."

"I *like* Spotty," Rosie went on. "When we play hide and seek he always wins because he is much harder to find than the rest of us. Don't you like him?"

"Of course we do," Mother Bunny replied. "We love Spotty. He just looks different – that's all."

"What's 'different,' Mum?"

"Stop asking questions, Rosie. Go and call the others. It's time for dinner."

For dinner they had lettuce and carrots. Now they were all in bed waiting for Mother Bunny to say good night.

"I heard Mum and Aunt Eliza talk about Spotty," Rosie began. "Aunt Eliza didn't like his spots. I wonder why?"

"I like my spots," Spotty said. "I think I look pretty."

"Yes, you are pretty," Rosie said. "And Mum said she loved you, you just looked different."

"What's different?" Spotty asked.

"I don't know myself," Rosie said.

Just then Mother Bunny came in.

"What's wrong with brown spots, Mum?" Rosie asked.

"Why, nothing – nothing's wrong with them!" Mother Bunny replied.

"And what does 'different' mean, Mum?"

"Stop asking questions, Rosie. It's time to sleep now. Tomorrow is Grandpa's birthday and we'll have to get up early to go to his birthday party." And Mother Bunny kissed all the bunnies good night.

197

They were getting ready for the party when Aunt Eliza came and took Mother Bunny aside. "How about Spotty?" she asked. "My advice is to leave him home."

"Why — I could not possibly!" Mother Bunny exclaimed.

"You know how upset Grandpa would be if he saw Spotty," Aunt Eliza said. "Do you want to spoil his birthday party?"

"I don't know what to do," Mother Bunny said weakly.

"I don't want to hurt Spotty . . ."

"But you certainly don't intend to spoil the day for Grandpa and all the family," Aunt Eliza said firmly. Mother Bunny finally gave in. So she had to go and tell Spotty that he was to stay

home. "It's just because of your brown spots," she said. "I'm so afraid that Grandpa may not like you as well as the others. I wish we could take you, Spotty, but we'll bring you something nice from the party."

"But Mum, you can't leave Spotty home all alone!" Rosie cried.

"He'll have a nice quiet day at home," Mother Bunny said, kissing Spotty good-bye. Spotty could not say a word. And then they all left and Spotty was alone.

Spotty did not even touch his breakfast. (And usually he
could eat all day long.) So he had to stay home because of those
spots of his! And he had thought he was pretty! But maybe he
could get rid of the spots. Spotty went to get the bottle of spot
remover. No – it didn't work. What now? Spotty thought and
thought – and then it came to him. He would run away, that was
the thing to do. It would make it easier for Mum, and maybe for
him too.

He would write a letter to let them know and then he would go.

"Dear Mum," he began. "I love you all but I have to leave you.
Maybe sometime. . . ."

Here he did not know how to go on, so he just signed his
name and put the letter on the table. Then he started to leave
but turned back at the door.

"I better take my breakfast along," he thought.

And then he really left.

It was getting dark. Spotty had roamed the woods all day
long. At first it had not been so bad, in fact rather like a picnic.
But now it had begun to rain and he felt tired and lonesome
and a little scared. Where should he spend the night? Maybe
he would go home after all. But no — he had left that letter. . . .
Spotty sat down under a tree, feeling very sad.

"Good evening, sir," somebody said.

Spotty looked up.

There was another rabbit standing right in front of him.

"Nasty weather, isn't it," the rabbit said. "I just came out for a little air."

Spotty stared at the newcomer. He had brown spots all over and blue eyes. He looked just like Spotty, only bigger.

"You seem rather tired," the rabbit said. "Come in and meet the family. My name is Brown."

"Mine is Spotty. How do you do, sir," Spotty said.

All the Browns looked like Mr. Brown, brown spots all over and blue eyes.

"This is Spotty. I met him in the woods," Mr. Brown said. "And these are my children."

They said hello to Spotty. They were all gay and happy. They did not seem to mind their spots a bit. Spotty began to feel quite at home. He looked around curiously. And then he discovered one more bunny. It was hiding in one corner and nobody seemed to take notice of it.

It was all white with pink eyes and a pink nose.

"Who is that?" Spotty gasped.

Mr. Brown lowered his voice.

"That's Whitie. She is . . . well, she is not quite like we are."

Spotty's mouth was wide open.

"Grandma has never seen Whitie at all," Mr. Brown went on. "She is so proud of the family — everyone with those pretty spots. She would be upset if she saw Whitie. It worries me very much."

"I can't understand this!" Spotty suddenly burst out. "I have got to tell you something important. My family looks just like Whitie, every single one of them. And Mum did not take me to Grandpa's birthday party because I have spots, like you all. So I

ran away from home. And now I come here and everything is the other way around. I just don't understand it!"

There was a long silence and they all seemed puzzled.

"That does seem strange indeed," Mr. Brown said finally, "your family not liking Spotties and our family not . . ."

"But I *do* like Whitie, I always did!" one of the bunnies broke in. "I only thought the others . . ."

"But we *all* like Whitie!" the other bunnies began to shout. "We only thought that Daddy . . ."

"Who said I did not like her! I've always loved Whitie!" Mr. Brown interrupted them. "I was only afraid that Grandma wouldn't, because Whitie looks different.

"But then — why shouldn't she look different? It all seems pretty foolish when I come to think of it."

They got Whitie out of her corner then and hugged and kissed her.

"Whitie looks so cute . . . just like Rosie," Spotty said dreamily.

"I always thought I was pretty," Whitie said. "And I never could understand what it was all about. I'm so happy you came, Spotty."

"And now to bed!" Mr. Brown said. "Tomorrow is another day. Spotty, I'll show you to your room. Good night and happy dreams."

Spotty was much too excited to sleep. So much had happened since that morning. First it had seemed as if this would be the worst day in his life — but now it looked as if things might still turn out all right. Spotty felt like running home this very minute to tell Mum and Rosie all about it. . . .

And then Spotty had a wonderful dream: There was an enormous table with carrots and carrots and carrots. And bunnies were sitting all around it, so many that he could not count them, spotties and white ones, big ones and small ones, and Spotty himself was sitting right in the middle of them and they were as happy as bunnies can be. . . .

But that was just a dream and not many dreams come true.

It was late when
Mother Bunny and her children
came home from Grandpa's birthday party.
"I wonder whether Spotty is still up," Mother Bunny said.
"I'll run inside and see," Rosie replied and went off. She was back in a minute. "I can't find him," she said. So they all started to look for him, but Spotty was not there.

And then they found the letter.

Mother Bunny read it and big tears began to run down her coat. "My little Spotty has run away!" she cried. "Oh, I wish I had not left him home alone. What am I going to do!"

"We will all go and look for him," Rosie suggested.

"It's too dark now, we'll have to wait until tomorrow," Mother Bunny said, wiping the tears off her eyes (her coat was all wet by now). "My poor little Spotty! . . ." "Don't worry, Mum, we'll find him tomorrow," Rosie said. But she was worried herself.

Mother Bunny just couldn't go to bed. When all the little
ones had fallen asleep, she tiptoed out of the house all by
herself. The night was cold and dark and Mother Bunny was
scared. But she *had* to find Spotty.

She wandered about for hours looking everywhere, calling
out his name. But she could not find him. There was no Spotty.

It was a lovely morning. The rain had washed the faces of the flowers clean and they were smiling at the sun. But Mother Bunny did not smile.

"Hurry up, all of you, and get ready to look for Spotty," she said, "while I prepare some food to take along for him." And she went down to the cellar.

The eight bunnies were all set to go now and they were standing among the flowers in the meadow, waiting for Mother Bunny to come.

Suddenly Rosie jumped high into the air.

"Look over there!" she shouted, pointing towards the woods. "I see something coming – and it looks like lots of Spotties!"

And that's what it was.

The Browns had gotten up bright and early that morning and they

were on their way to see Spotty home and to meet his family.

"Mum, Mum, come quick!" Rosie shouted.

Mother Bunny rushed up – and then she could not believe her eyes. The whole meadow was full of Spotties, and among them one little white bunny. And ahead of them all, safe and sound, was her own Spotty.

"Spotty!" she cried, and then he was in her arms and she hugged and kissed him. Then it was Rosie's turn and then came all the others and it was quite a while before Spotty could breathe again.

"This is Mr. Brown and his family," he said finally. Then he began to tell all that had happened last night, and that was a lot. Everybody listened in silence and when he had ended Mother Bunny did not quite know whether to cry or to laugh. "Why, I don't

216

know *what* to say," she said and
turned to Mr. Brown. "You know, I always
loved Spotty just as much as the others, but I was only afraid
that Grandpa . . ."

"But that's precisely what all of us were saying!" Mr. Brown
said, and then they all burst out laughing.

"Well, I guess we were just a little foolish," Mother Bunny
said. "But it's all over now. Oh, I am so happy!" And she gave
Mr. Brown a big kiss and then everybody kissed everybody and
everybody asked everybody's name and everybody laughed and
danced and sang and the noise could be heard three miles away.

And then they had a big party. There was an enormous table
with carrots and carrots and carrots. And bunnies were sitting all
around it, so many that you could not count them, spotties and

white ones, big ones and small ones, and Spotty was sitting right
in the middle of them and they were as happy as bunnies can be.
Not many dreams come true – but Spotty's did!

The End

Billy's Picture

by

Margret & H. A. Rey

"I want to draw a picture,"
said Billy the Bunny.

So he took a pencil and began to draw. Just then Penny the Puppy happened to come along.

"That's a pretty picture," said Penny.
"But it needs a HEAD. Please let me do it."
And he took the pencil and drew a head with
long floppy ears just like his own.

"There you are," he said. "That's the way it should be." "But. . . ." Billy began. Just then Greta the Goose happened to come along.

"That's a lovely picture," said Greta.
"But it needs FEET. Please let me do them."
And she took the pencil and drew a pair of
feet just like her own.

"There you are," she said. "That's the way it should be." "But what. . . ." Billy began. Just then Paul the Porcupine happened to come along.

"That's a wonderful picture," said Paul.
"But it needs QUILLS. Please let me do
them." And he took the pencil and drew lots
and lots of quills just like his own.

"There you are," he said. "That's the way it should be." "But what I. . . ." Billy began. Just then Ronny the Rooster happened to come along.

"That's a beautiful picture," said Ronny.
"But it needs a COMB. Please let me do it."
And he took the pencil and drew a comb
just like his own.

"There you are," he said. "That's the way
it should be." "But what I wanted...." Billy
began. Just then Oliver the Owl happened
to come along.

"That's a great picture," said Oliver.
"But it needs WINGS. Please let me do
them." And he took the pencil and drew a
pair of wings just like his own.

"There you are," he said. "That's the way it should be." "But what I wanted to. . . ." Billy began. Just then Maggie the Mouse happened to come along.

"That's a sweet picture," said Maggie. "But it needs a TAIL. Please let me do it." And she took the pencil and drew a tail just like her own.

"There you are," she said. "That's the way it should be." "But what I wanted to draw...." Billy began.

Just then Eric the Elephant happened to come along. "That's a delightful picture," said Eric. "But it needs a TRUNK. Please let me do it."

**And he took the pencil and drew a trunk
just like his own. "There you are," he said.
"That's the way it should be."**

"But what I wanted to draw." Billy began once more —and this time nobody happened to come along—"what I wanted to draw isn't a PUPPYGOOSE or a PORCUPHANT or whatever you call this silly picture. All I wanted to draw was a picture of myself!"

Here Billy began to cry and for a moment nobody said anything. Then everybody started to talk at the same time.

"A picture of myself— that's just what I wanted to do!" said Penny and Greta and Paul and Ronny and Oliver and Eric.

Billy stopped crying. "Why not do it then?" he said.

**And that's what they did: Eric drew an
elephant and Maggie drew a mouse. Paul
drew a porcupine and Greta drew a goose.**

Penny drew a puppy and Oliver drew an owl. Ronny drew a rooster—and can you guess what Billy drew?

That's what he drew!

Whiteblack the Penguin
Sees the World

MARGRET & H. A. REY

WHITEBLACK THE PENGUIN was worried. He was the Chief Storyteller on Station W-O-N-S. Spelled backwards it read S-N-O-W, the radio station for all Penguinland. And he had run out of stories.

"I guess I'll take a vacation and travel," he said. "Travelers always have lots of stories."

His friends Seal and Polar Bear agreed.

"But you'll need a boat," said Seal. "You can't swim all the time. I'll give you half of an old seal skin. It will make a fine boat."

"And I," said Polar Bear, "I'll give you rope made from the hair of my last winter's fur. Ropes are always useful."

"That's wonderful," said Whiteblack. "Besides, I've always wanted a boat and a rope."

So he began to build the boat, and with all the family helping, it was finished in no time. Whiteblack was ready for his trip.

Everybody waved farewell to him.

"Come back with plenty of stories!" barked Seal.

"And bring us nice presents!" said Polar Bear.

"I promise!" shouted Whiteblack. "Good-bye!"

The boat moved away from the shore, and soon he was alone on the wide blue ocean.

Hours went by and not much happened. Sometimes Whiteblack swam pulling the boat behind him, and sometimes he sat in the boat using his flippers as paddles.

"I thought traveling was more exciting," he said. Feeling bored, he fell asleep.

CRACK! He awoke to a heavy shock. His boat had hit an iceberg! It was sinking fast. "I hate to lose my boat," he said, "but at least this is a story for my radio show. Besides, I've always wanted to be in an accident."

He untied the
rope just as the boat
went under. He then
tied it around his middle
and swam on.

After a while Whiteblack
saw smoke on the horizon:
there was a cruiser steaming
straight toward him.

"I'll go on board and look at
this ship," he said.

When the cruiser was close enough, he lassoed a gun and climbed on board.

Everything aboard the cruiser was clean and shiny, and Whiteblack was pleased. On deck was one of those famous human beings he had heard so much about!

"I've always wanted to see a man, but I thought he'd look more unusual," Whiteblack said. "Why, he looks just like me! White shirt, dark coat, and he walks on two legs. Only he's got lovely bright buttons on his jacket. I'll go ask him to let me have a few for my Sunday suit."

Just then the officer and some sailors discovered the little penguin and started chasing him. He ran away as fast as he could and hid in the muzzle of a big gun.

"I hope I'm safe here," he thought. "It's a nice cool place for a *long* nap."

The next morning the sailors started practicing with the gun
where Whiteblack was sleeping. BOOM! He went through the air
like a thunderbolt, and miles away he dived into the sea.

"This is a *real* story for my radio show!" he said when he came up. "Besides, I've always wanted to fly."

He saw land in the distance and swam ashore.

"This must be a foreign country." He climbed up the beach. "I suppose it's full of stories for my radio show. Besides, I've always wanted to visit a foreign country."

The place was quite different from Penguinland. There was no snow or ice, but there were bright flowers and fresh green plants everywhere. The air was warm, a little too warm for Whiteblack's taste.

But look at the two big white balls lying there! They couldn't be snowballs . . . or could they?

"Perhaps footballs," he thought. "Besides, I've always wanted to play football." He kicked one ball with his foot.

CRICK! The ball broke in two and out came a baby ostrich.

"Thanks for letting me out of the egg," he squeaked. "Won't you please get my brother out, too?"

So Whiteblack hit the second egg and another baby ostrich appeared.

"I've always wanted to see baby ostriches come out of their eggs," Whiteblack said. "It's a very rare experience and a fine story for my radio show."

That moment Father and Mother Ostrich arrived. "What a pleasant surprise," they said. "Won't you accept a little present?" Mother Ostrich gave him a lovely mirror, and Father Ostrich produced a roller skate.

"Thanks," said Whiteblack. "Now I must go because I'm on a trip, collecting stories for my radio show."

"Wait," said Father Ostrich. "The desert is hard to travel for somebody with such short legs — pardon me for saying so. I'll give you a letter of introduction to my friend the camel. He'll let you ride on his back."

Whiteblack took the letter and walked into the desert. It was like the beach in Penguinland, only warmer. Soon he met the camel.

The camel was very glad to have company, for the desert is such a lonely place. "I provide the ferry service across the desert," the camel said, "and I charge a small fee, but because of that letter I shall carry you for free."

The camel knelt down and Whiteblack climbed on its back. "Another good story for my radio show," he said. "Besides, I've always wanted to ride on a camel."

At first Whiteblack liked the ride, but after a while he had a funny feeling in his stomach.

With every step the camel's back moved up and down, up and
down, and he felt he was going to be seasick. "This would *not* make
a good story for my radio show," he thought, "and besides, I *never*
wanted to be seasick. Penguins are not *supposed* to be seasick, ever!

Finally he could not stand it anymore. He asked the camel to
please let him off.

Now he had to walk through the hot desert again, for hours and hours.

"I wish I were home," he sighed. "Besides, I've never wanted to be lost in a desert. I must get out of here somehow." Suddenly he had an idea. He picked up a stick and with his rope he tied it to the roller skate. It made a perfect scooter! It even had a rearview mirror.

He rolled along smoothly all the way to the end of the desert.

"Now I've got enough stories for my radio show," he decided. "I want to go home. If I only knew which way to go. Why, there's a plane over there. Maybe there's somebody who can tell me how to get back to Penguinland."

And there was! An explorer was quite surprised to see the little penguin. "I'm leaving tomorrow," he said, "and I can give you a lift."

The explorer made a little carrier for Whiteblack. And because no animals were allowed inside the plane, the carrier was fastened on top.

"I've always wanted to ride on top of an airplane," said Whiteblack. "Now I'm on my way home!"

The plane took off and flew over towns and rivers and fields and forests and finally it reached the ocean.

"It's getting cooler," thought Whiteblack. "I can feel we are coming closer to Penguinland. I must try to have a look. Besides, I've always wanted to have a look at Penguinland from the air."

He managed to open the door of his carrier and walked out to have a better view.

He bent over and SWOOSH! Down he went, headfirst, and SPLASH! he plumped into the sea.

When he recovered from his fall he looked around. He was curious. There were fish right and left and everywhere; he had never seen so many fish in his life.

Suddenly he and all the fish were lifted out of the water. He had fallen into a fishing net, and the net was being pulled in. Together with everybody else, Whiteblack was dumped into the hold of a fishing boat.

"Not a bad place," he said to himself. "Lots of fish, lots of ice, just the right temperature. Now I can make up for all the meals I've missed during my trip."

So he had ten breakfasts, ten lunches, ten dinners, and ten suppers, all in one, and every course was fish. He was just ready for a nap when he heard a fisherman upstairs say, "Over there lies Penguinland!"

Penguinland! He was almost home and yet he had no present for his friends. "I must bring *something*," he said. "What can I do?" And then a wonderful idea came to him.

At night when everybody was asleep he climbed on deck. He took one of the big nets that were hung up to dry and jumped into the sea.

His idea worked! As he swam toward Penguinland, dragging the net behind him, fish were caught in it. Soon the net became quite heavy. "I don't mind," he thought. "I'm on my way home, with stories to tell and a *marvelous* present!"

The morning came and he could see the shores of Penguinland far away, but the net was so heavy now that he hardly made any headway. "I *must* get home with my present," he panted. "I MUST!"

But his strength was almost gone.
He would have to let the net go
and come home empty-handed.
He just had to give up! Tears
were coming to his eyes . . .

"Whiteblack! Hello, Whiteblack!" shouted a happy voice. It was Seal, his good friend Seal, who came rushing through the waves to help him. "I've been looking out for you every day. I'm *so* glad you are back! What a *marvelous* present you brought!" And he took the heavy load from Whiteblack.

HURRAH! There was a big crowd on the beach to welcome the famous traveler. That same day they had an enormous party with mountains of fish for everybody. Whiteblack had a special radio show on Station W-O-N-S, and he had to tell all his stories over and over again.

And out of snow his friends built a big monument and wrote on it: WHITEBLACK, THE HERO OF PENGUINLAND.

And since in Penguinland the snow never melts, the monument is still there. You can go yourself and see it.

> "Not all our children's books are about George,
> but they are all about animals. We both loved them."
> —MARGRET REY

A Few Notes about *Curious George and Friends*

Curious George

Curious George and his creators had quite a journey getting to America. In 1940, before dawn on a rainy day in June, Hans and Margret left Paris just hours before the Nazis invaded the city. On bicycles that Hans had pieced together, they headed to the French-Spanish border, carrying very little with them besides a few treasured manuscripts and artwork, including *Curious George*. They went by train to Lisbon, then on to Rio de Janeiro, arriving finally in New York City in October of the same year, where they took a small apartment in Greenwich Village and rolled up their sleeves. "Before the week was over, we had found a home for Curious George at Houghton Mifflin," Margret later wrote. Their editor at Houghton Mifflin, Grace Hogarth, was a familiar face, as she had published their books in England. In 1941, *Curious George* was published and slowly he has become known around the world as "Georges," "Zozo," "Bingo," "Nicke," "Peter Pedal," "Coco," and "Piete," among other names.

Cecily G. and the 9 Monkeys

Curious George makes his first appearance in this book about eight monkey children, their mother, and a playful giraffe. *Cecily G. and the 9 Monkeys* came about when an editor at the French publishing company Gallimard saw Mr. Rey's whimsical drawings of a giraffe in a French periodical and encouraged him to try his hand at a children's story. In 1939, the book was first published in France as *Rafi et les 9 Singes*. An English-language edition was published later that year in England as *Raffy and the 9 Monkeys*. In the American edition, published in 1942, Raffy's name became Cecily G. (G. for Giraffe), and the mischievous little monkey who was first known as Fifi became Curious George. You will notice in this first book that George talks, although he doesn't speak in future books. Here, he also has a mother: Mother Pamplemoose. And her littlest monkey is called Jinny, a name that the Reys later gave to one of their pet cocker spaniels.

Elizabite

First published in 1942 by Harper & Row and edited by the legendary Ursula Nordstrom, this early title was dedicated simply by Hans: "To Peggy." The flap copy on the original jacket provides a note about

Hans's inspiration: "When asked about the origin of Elizabite, Mr. Rey (who has spent many years in Brazil) told of an evening in Rio when he was dining with friends, among them a botanist who entertained the party with strange tales about carnivorous plants. Ever since, Mr. Rey has looked with suspicion at flower arrangements on dinner tables, and as the years went by he often tried to imagine what a carnivorous plant might develop into, under proper care. His thoughts on the subject crystallized into the colorful and energetic shape of Elizabite in the present book."

Pretzel

Pretzel, originally published in 1944, was the first book that credits Margret Rey as author. In answering how they worked together and who did what, Margret stated, "Basically H.A. illustrated and Margret wrote. But that is not the whole story. H.A. also had ideas, which Margret then turned into a story. And Margret sometimes wrote her own books, such as *Pretzel* and *Spotty,* and H.A. did the illustrations, at times changing the story a little to fit his pictures." Though they wrote the books in partnership, Margret had been resigned for many years to accepting the gender-free, somewhat mysterious "H.A." to stand as the author credit on the Curious George books. It was on her insistence that her name appeared, finally, on *Curious George Flies a Kite* in 1958.

Margret and Hans's editor at Harper, Ursula Nordstrom, challenged the team to create a small book, an inventive way to conserve paper during the war: hence the small format of the original book as well as the single piece of art that wraps around the jacket. A sequel to *Pretzel,* called *Pretzel and the Puppies,* was presented as a series of stories in a format similar to that of a comic strip. Many of these stories were published in *Good Housekeeping* magazine in the late 1940s. Pretzel inspired a balloon that appeared in a Macy's Thanksgiving Day Parade, and, along with Spotty, Katy No-Pocket, and George, he has also made an appearance as a plush toy.

Katy No-Pocket

Descended from a long line of writers, Emmy Payne wrote and cowrote several books. She is best known to young readers, however, for her story about a mother kangaroo who cleverly finds a solution to the problem of not having a pocket. H. A. Rey enriched the story with illustrations in watercolors that are similar to those used in his books about Curious George. Young readers may notice that the street scene in *Katy No-Pocket* looks like one in which Curious George could have felt right at home—complete with smiling cars and trucks and a woman out for a stroll with her black cocker spaniel.

Spotty

Spotty, first published in 1945, might have been partly inspired by Margret's childhood fondness for a set of toy bunnies covered with real fur. But it was also inspired by race relations in the country in the 1940s and her and Hans's friendship with the African American educator and author Jesse Jackson, whom they met at the Bread Loaf Writers' Conference. Margret was also a mentor and editor to Jackson, whose works include *Call Me Charley* and a biography of Mahalia Jackson. The Reys' belief that people can be different and still live together in harmony is a theme that recurs in a small wordless book for adults called *Zebrology*, published by Chatto & Windus in London, which illustrates Hans's fantastical interpretation of the evolution of the zebra from both white and black horses.

Billy's Picture

Billy's Picture was first published by Harper and Brothers in 1948. The story was quite popular, as editions were published in a variety of languages, including German, Japanese, Swedish, and Danish. In the mid-1960s, however, sales had slowed so much that when the Reys received a royalty statement in 1966, they thought the book must be out of print because the amount was so small. H.A.'s editor, Ursula Nordstrom, soon found a letter on her desk inquiring about the status of the book. It included a drawing of a rabbit reclining in the grass next to a tombstone that read: "Here Lies Billy, 1948–1965, R.I.P." With the Reys' encouragement, *Billy's Picture* was brought back into print with a new blue background color rather than the original lime green. The inclusion of *Billy's Picture* in this collection is also a celebration of the book coming back into print after a long rest.

Whiteblack the Penguin Sees the World

It was generally thought that the Reys had escaped from Paris, as mentioned, with only four manuscripts in their packs. But in 1999, when the publisher of Houghton Mifflin Children's Books, Anita Silvey, visited the Rey archive at the de Grummond Children's Literature Collection at the University of Southern Mississippi in Hattiesburg, she became aware of the unpublished manuscript. According to archived correspondence, *Whiteblack the Penguin* was submitted to Ursula Nordstrom at Harper and Brothers. A letter dated October 27, 1942, includes her comments: "I think *Whiteblack* can be shortened, sharpened, and improved. I hope you will let me see it again." But there is no written confirmation that the manuscript or illustrations were revised or submitted again. The original jacket illustration was marked with "Propriété de l'auteur H. A. Rey, Paris," indicating the Reys' address in France. Lay Lee Ong, a longtime friend of Margret Rey's and executor of the Rey estate, has noted that *Whiteblack* was inspired by Margret and Hans's days working at the 1937 Paris World's Fair in the Brazilian Pavilion, which was stationed across from a penguin exhibit. Hans spent his days drawing the delightful creatures, and he and Margret created characters out of them. The book was finally published in 2000.

Quotes from "About Margret and H. A. Rey and Curious George" by Margret Rey in *The Complete Adventures of Curious George.*